THE Berenstain BEAR SCOUTS
and the
Ice Monster

Look for more books in
The Berenstain Bear Scouts series:

*The Berenstain Bear Scouts
in Giant Bat Cave*

*The Berenstain Bear Scouts
and the Humongous Pumpkin*

*The Berenstain Bear Scouts
Meet Bigpaw*

*The Berenstain Bear Scouts
Save That Backscratcher*

*The Berenstain Bear Scouts
and the Terrible Talking Termite*

*The Berenstain Bear Scouts and the
Coughing Catfish*

*The Berenstain Bear Scouts and the
Sci-Fi Pizza*

*The Berenstain Bear Scouts
Ghost Versus Ghost*

*The Berenstain Bear Scouts
and the Sinister Smoke Ring*

*The Berenstain Bear Scouts
and the Magic Crystal Caper*

*The Berenstain Bear Scouts
and the Run-Amuck Robot*

THE Berenstain BEAR SCOUTS
and the
Ice Monster

by Stan & Jan Berenstain
Illustrated by Michael Berenstain

A
LITTLE APPLE
PAPERBACK

SCHOLASTIC INC.
New York Toronto London Auckland Sydney

No part of this publication may be reproduced in whole or in part, or stored in a retrieval system, or transmitted in any form or by any means, electronic, mechanical, photocopying, recording, or otherwise, without written permission of the publisher. For information regarding permission, write to Scholastic Inc., 555 Broadway, New York, NY 10012.

ISBN 0-590-94479-7

12 11 10 9 8 7 6 5 4 3 2   7 8 9/9 0 1 2/0

Printed in the U.S.A.   40

First Scholastic printing, December 1997

• Table of Contents •

1. Grand Marshal Papa 1
2. Warning from a Stranger 5
3. Great Plans 9
4. A Double Mission 15
5. A Present for Bigpaw 19
6. A Cry for Help 29
7. Freezing and Starving! 35
8. Please, Papa, Have a Heart! 45
9. The Crystal Tower 48
10. A Message on Snow Mountain 54
11. Ralph on Ice 59
12. Awfully Early for Screaming and Hollering 63
13. The Doomsday Monster 67
14. In Bigpaw's Cave 74
15. A Big Target 79
16. You Win Some, You Lose Some 89

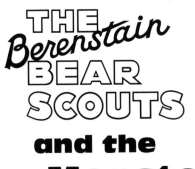

THE Berenstain BEAR SCOUTS
and the
Ice Monster

• Chapter 1 •

Grand Marshal Papa

There it was, right there in the newspaper: PAPA Q. BEAR NAMED GRAND MARSHAL OF THE WINTER CARNIVAL. Papa was as pleased as punch and twice as proud. So were the Bear Scouts.

"May we help, Papa? May we? Please?" cried the scouts.

"Of course you may," said the newly named Grand Marshal grandly. "I hereby appoint the 'one for all and all for one!' Bear Scouts as my official deputies."

Papa had a right to be proud, the scouts had a right to be excited, and Mama had a

right to be a little worried. The Beartown
Ice Carnival was a truly great event, and
being its Grand Marshal was a big responsibility. Bears came from all over Bear
Country to see its sights, ride its rides,
and take part in its competitions.

And what glorious sights they were!
One year the main attraction was a huge
snowbear that stood at the entrance to the
carnival. To enter, guests had to go
through the great arch of the giant snowbear's legs. Another year the main attraction was a reconstruction of the Ice Age
with life-size sculptures of the last of the
dinosaurs.

And what rides! The Ice Carnival offered rides galore: tobogganing, iceboating, snowmobiling!

As for the competitions, you name it, the Ice Carnival had it! There was speed skating, figure skating, ski jumping, and barrel jumping!

But it was more than the sights, rides, and competitions that brought the bears of Bear Country to the Ice Carnival. It was the chance to take part in the great spirit of winter. It hadn't always been so. In earlier times, winter had been a long, bleak, dreary season. Bears had huddled joylessly and wandered aimlessly across the frozen wastes with nothing to look forward to but the faint hope of a distant spring. In much, much earlier times, the bears hadn't even huddled. They'd hibernated.

But that was then, and this was now. And the bears of Beartown were arriving at Town Hall to hear the official announcement of Papa's appointment as Grand Marshal of the Winter Carnival.

• Chapter 2 •

Warning from a Stranger

"Wow!" said Sister as the scouts joined the crowd moving toward Town Hall. "This is some crowd!"

Sister was right. Everybody who was anybody seemed to be there. There was also somebody who wasn't anybody the scouts had ever seen before. They certainly would have remembered if they had. He wore a raggedy hat, a raggedy suit, and a raggedy beard.

"He sure is strange-looking," said Fred.

"Scary-looking is more like it," said Lizzy.

"Look. He's handing out little cards," said Brother.

"Maybe he'll give me one," said Sister, scurrying off through the crowd.

"Hey, wait!" said Brother, who was always nervous about Sister's bold ways. Not that there was much anybody could do about it. That's the way it was with the Bear Scouts. Each scout brought something special to the troop. Sister was bold. Brother was a natural leader. Super-smart Fred read the dictionary and encyclopedia just for fun. Lizzy was so in tune with nature that she could pet a skunk

without getting skunked.

Sister was threading her way back, reading a little card. "Weird," she said as she rejoined the troop.

"You didn't need a card to figure that out," said Fred.

"No," said Sister. "That's his name: I. M. Weird!"

"What's the card say?" asked Brother.

"See for yourself," said Sister as she handed Brother the card.

Fred and Lizzy looked over Brother's shoulder as he read the card. This is what it said:

REPENT! Or prepare to meet your DOOM!

"Hoo-ie!" said Fred.

"It's enough to give you the shivers," said Lizzy.

"Repent of what?" said Brother.

"Modern ways," said Gramps, who had been listening nearby. "He passes through here every winter. He's dead set against modern ways. He's especially against the Winter Carnival — says it's against nature. Wants us to go back to the old ways."

"What's he want us to do?" asked Brother.

"Hibernate," said Gramps.

"Hibernate?" said Fred.

"Yep," said Gramps. "He's a hiberna-tionist."

They had reached the Town Hall door and were about to enter. "Weird," said Brother.

"No," said Sister. "I. M. Weird."

• Chapter 3 •
Great Plans

"Speaking of hibernation," said Fred as the troop looked for good seats, "let's not forget Bigpaw."

Bigpaw was the giant throwback to prehistoric cavebears that the scouts and Professor Actual Factual had discovered on a fossil hunt. The scouts were friendly with Bigpaw and kept in touch with him. Bigpaw still lived in the Great Grizzly Mountains and, of course, hibernated. They had a present for Bigpaw and planned to take it to him as a sort of hibernation gift.

"Shh!" said Brother. "The mayor is about to begin."

It took a little while for the town meeting to quiet down. Many of Papa's friends and neighbors had seen the announcement in the newspaper and were congratulating him on his appointment as Grand Marshal.

"Friet, quiends — er, quiet, friends," said Mayor Honeypot, tapping the microphone. The citizens of Beartown were used to the fact that the mayor sometimes got the fronts and backs of his words mixed up. So they just waited patiently until he got them straightened out.

"Cellow fitizens — er, fellow citizens — we are hathered gere — er, gathered here — to announce that the Grand Marshal of this year's Winter Carnival is that brince among pears — er, prince among bears — none other than Baba Q. Pear, er, Quapa P. Bear, er, Papa B. Quear . . ."

The mayor never did get Papa's name out properly, but it really didn't matter because the crowd was on its feet giving Papa a standing ovation. The scouts were very proud. So was Mama, though she was still nervous about the responsibility Papa was taking on.

But there was one member of the audience who was not cheering, applauding, or standing. It was the raggedy stranger.

The cry of "Speech! Speech!" went up. Papa clasped his hands over his head like

a winning boxer and bounded onto the stage. When the applause died down he took hold of the microphone. "Mr. Mayor, friends, and neighbors," he said. "I am proud to accept the appointment as Grand Marshal of the Beartown Winter Carnival. I have great plans. This year's carnival will have the most exciting rides and the most demanding competitions. For the main attraction I will build a mighty and magnificent tower of ice. Yes, friends, this year's Winter Carnival will be the biggest and the best Winter Carnival in the history of Bear Country!"

Another cheer began to go up. But before it could get started, a voice rang out.

"And the last!"

A buzz of "huh?" "whozat?" and "whudysay?" ran through the crowd. It didn't take long for the audience to figure out it was the voice of the raggedy stranger — the one who had been handing out "doom" cards.

12

"The last what, sir?" asked Papa politely.

"Look," said Sister. "It's the hibernationist!"

"Shh!" said Brother. "I want to hear." All eyes were on the hibernationist.

"The last Winter Carnival, you fools! The Winter Carnival is against nature! Those who go against nature are doomed! Give up modern ways! Go back to the old ways! Hibernate! Only those who hibernate will be saved!"

The audience wasn't as polite as Papa. "Who's *that* nut?" "Who invited him?" "Throw him out!"

Mayor Honeypot took the microphone. "Sergeant at arms! Sergeant at arms! Please escort that pisruptive derson — er, disruptive person — out of here!"

Officer Marguerite was already hustling the doom-shouting stranger up the aisle. "Doomed! Doomed!" he cried. "You are all doomed! Repent of your wicked modern ways!"

Once outside, the stranger continued his warning. "Go back to the old ways! Hibernate! Only those who hibernate shall be saved! So says I. M. Weird!"

Officer Marguerite closed the door. But out of sight isn't always out of mind. The raggedy stranger's warning cast a spell of gloom over the Town Hall audience.

• Chapter 4 •

A Double Mission

But not for long. There was so much excitement about the Winter Carnival and so much to do to get ready for it that the bears of Beartown all but forgot about I. M. Weird's weird warnings. True, he showed up here and there and handed out his little cards. But he was merely a winter nuisance in the way mosquitoes are a summer nuisance.

Speaking of winter, it had come on strong since the town meeting. It had snowed almost steadily. Snow blanketed Beartown and the countryside. If the countryside was blanketed, the high mountains were triple-quilted. And it was cold! Every outdoor bear breath was punctuated with a puff of steam.

It was a good thing that winter had come on strong. Without a cold snowy winter it would have been very difficult for Grand Marshal Papa to put on the biggest and best Winter Carnival in the history of Bear Country. The thick snow would not only provide plenty of material for the snow-sculpture contest, it promised good tobogganing, skiing, and snowmobiling.

Zero temperatures were even more important to Papa's plans. The centerpiece of the carnival was to be the great ice tower Papa had mentioned at the town meeting. Without zero temperatures he would not be able to carry out his plan to build the tower with blocks of ice cut from the frozen surface of Lake Grizzly.

Mama couldn't help worrying. Papa

did sometimes have a tendency to get carried away. But not this time. He was taking his responsibilities as Grand Marshal very seriously. He knew winter carnivals were big business. So he called Squire Grizzly, the richest bear in Bear Country, for business advice. Food would be needed at the Winter Carnival. Papa called on the managers of The Burger Bear and the Pizza Shack for help.

One of the complaints at last year's carnival was the lack of hot drinks. Beartown Dairies agreed to have a tank car of hot cocoa at the carnival. Papa knew that big events like the Winter Carnival often attracted pickpockets and petty crooks. Chief of Police Bruno told Papa not to worry. He planned to hire extra officers to help him and Officer Marguerite police the Winter Carnival.

There was also Dr. Gert Grizzly, head of Beartown Hospital. The Winter Carnival was held for the benefit of the hospital, so wise Dr. Gert was always available for advice.

And, of course, there were Papa's official deputies, the Bear Scouts. They were all over the place helping: carrying messages, running errands, and helping plan the competitions. At this very moment Papa's deputies were snowshoeing up the side of Mount Grizzly. They were on a double mission. They were marking out the toboggan and ski runs, and they were taking Bigpaw his hibernation present.

• Chapter 5 •

A Present for Bigpaw

The scouts stopped for a rest before pressing on to Bigpaw's winter cave. It had been a long, tough climb. Especially with downhill skis and poles strapped to their backs. Brother had the extra job of carrying Bigpaw's present. It wasn't very heavy, but it was bulky and awkward.

"Phew!" said Fred. "It's a good thing we don't have to climb to Bigpaw's summer cave."

"You've got that right!" said Brother.

"Look! There he is!" called Sister.

"*Yo, Bigpaw!*" shouted the scouts, waving and speeding up as much as their high-stepping snowshoe walk allowed. Bigpaw saw them and waved. A huge smile split the giant's face. And giant he was. With shoulders like boulders, arms like tree trunks, and paws like Dumpsters.

"We made it just in time!" said Lizzy. "He's gathering brush and straw for his hibernation bed."

"A good thing," said Brother. "Once he's into his winter sleep, you couldn't wake him with an earthquake."

Even though the scouts had helped Professor Actual Factual discover Bigpaw, every time they visited they were shocked all over again at his great bulk and towering height. And when he swept them up, snowshoes, skis, and all, in his mighty arms, they were reminded once again of his great strength and gentle nature.

"Bigpaw miss cubs. Glad you come see him." He had gathered them up in a mass of brush and straw, and it was tickling their noses.

"We're glad to see you, too," said Brother.

"Yes," said Lizzy. "And we've brought you a present."

"Present? Oh, boy!" said Bigpaw. "Bigpaw love presents. You give Bigpaw present now."

"As soon as you put us down," said Brother.

Bigpaw carried them into his winter cave and gently put them down. Then he carried the brush and straw to the rear of the cave. Bigpaw's winter cave was enormous — much bigger than his summer cave at the top of Mount Grizzly. He'd fixed it up a bit since the scouts' last visit. Bigpaw had made a table out of a great slab of rock. He had found a boulder that was shaped sort of like an easy chair. It had a foot rock in front of it. The only other things in the cave were his tree-size, one-string banjo and his hibernation bed of brush and straw.

"You certainly have fixed your cave up nicely," said Lizzy.

"Thank you. Bigpaw like things be nice," he said. "But where present? Bigpaw want present."

"Here it is, big guy!" said Brother.

Bigpaw reached down and took the package in his enormous paws. Then he took it to his slab table, sat in his rock chair, carefully undid the ribbon, and gently removed the tissue. Bigpaw gasped when he saw the present. It was a large teddy bear with a beautiful red bow. Bigpaw's eyes sparkled when he saw it. "A teddy!" he said. "Bigpaw love teddy. Bigpaw need teddy for company." He hugged it to his cheek and rocked gently.

"It's a hibernation present," said Sister. "You know, for you to hug during your long winter sleep."

Bigpaw was beginning to get sleepy, and the word "sleep" triggered an enormous yawn. It shook the cave and echoed out through the mountains, causing snowslides.

"Hi-ber-nation?" said Bigpaw. "What hiber-nation?"

"It's what you do in the winter," said

Fred. "You know, sleep through the winter."

Another big yawn. More shaking. More snowslides.

"It's kind of a special sleep," continued Fred. "All bears used to do it. But modern bears don't."

"We sort of got out of the habit," said Brother.

"Yeah," said Lizzy. "And there's this guy who says we *should* do it."

"And if we don't, something awful is going to happen," added Sister.

Bigpaw frowned. "This guy want to hurt scouts?" he said.

"It's nothing serious," said Brother.

"If he hurt scouts, Bigpaw chew him up and spit him out." Bigpaw acted out chewing somebody up and spitting him out. It was frightening to see. "Bigpaw squash bad guy like grape," said Bigpaw. He brought his gigantic fist down hard on the table. If it hadn't been solid rock, it would have been smashed to pieces.

"Hey, it's okay, big guy," said Brother. "Nothing to worry about. Why, I haven't even seen the guy around town for a couple of weeks. Well, we've got to go. We've got work to do."

"What kind of work?" said Bigpaw.

"We're marking off routes for the carnival. You know — toboggan slides, ski runs. That sort of thing."

"What is carn-i-val?" asked Bigpaw.

"The Winter Carnival," said Brother. "But, hey. That's right. You're always hibernating when the Winter Carnival is on. It's like a great big party. It has rides, music, all kinds of contests and art shows. It's terrific! And this year Papa is going to build a great tower of ice. Oh, yeah! The Winter Carnival is really great! Well, so long, Bigpaw! Pleasant dreams!"

The scouts put on their downhill skis

and got ready to go back down the mountain. Bigpaw suppressed a yawn and went back into his cave. Hugging his teddy close, he climbed into his bed of brush and straw and fell fast asleep.

As for Bigpaw's dreams, they would be more than pleasant. That hibernation season, mighty Bigpaw's dreams would shake the very earth.

• Chapter 6 •

A Cry for Help

The scouts were ready for their downhill run. They pushed off with their ski poles and sped down the mountain. Down they whizzed, leaving blue dye markers as they went. When the ground flattened out, they stopped to tighten their backpacks, then set out cross-country.

In the summer the stretch that lay before them was a beautiful patchwork of greens: the grassy green of fields and meadows, the dark green of Farmer Ben's cornfields, the orange-flecked green of his pumpkin patch, the rich green of his orchards, and beyond Ben's farm the rough green of the woods that bordered the river. But now, in the dead of winter, everything was white.

It was snowing steadily now. The snow-shoe prints they had made on their way were already snowed under. The three sentinels stood just ahead. They were three huge boulders that were said to guard Mount Grizzly. They were the only things in sight that weren't completely snow-covered. As the scouts shussed forward in the silent snow, they felt as if they were the only living beings on a strange planet where no one had gone before.

But as they approached the first sentinel, it became clear that someone *had* gone there before. They not only had gone there, they'd written something on the sentinels! Graffiti on the sentinels? The scouts were outraged! Who could have done such a thing? But wait. It wasn't graffiti, it was a message. *A message for them!*

The first sentinel said, "A message for the Bear Scouts." The second said, "On a matter of life or death!" The third said, "Help!" and it was signed "Ralph R." There was no question who "Ralph R." was. It was Ralph Ripoff, Beartown's notorious crook, swindler, pickpocket, and petty thief.

The message from Ralph was a little confusing. Everyone knew that Ralph headed south in the winter. He simply sailed his houseboat down the river to warmer climes and practiced his trade of cheating and stealing in southern Bear Country until spring.

So there were questions about how and why the message got there. But the main question was what to do about it. It was a strange place to have a scout meeting — out in the swirling snow in the middle of nowhere. But have a scout meeting they did.

"This meeting of the Bear Scouts will come to order," said Brother.

"Hey! Never mind that stuff!" said Sister. "I'm freezing!"

A MESSAGE FOR THE BEAR SCOUTS—

"The question before the house," said Brother, who liked things to be done correctly, "is what to do about this message."

"What house?" said Fred. "We're standing here in a blinding snowstorm!"

"The message says it's a matter of life and death!" said Lizzy.

"You've got a point," said Brother. "Even Ralph wouldn't say 'life or death' if he wasn't in real trouble."

"Then let's investigate!" said Sister, poling off cross-country toward Great Roaring River. Though it wasn't roaring at the moment. It was as quiet as ice.

As they emerged from the woods that bordered the river, they saw Ralph's houseboat. It was frozen in solid, all but caged with icicles. Hmmm, thought Brother, this looks as though it could be serious.

Even though Ralph was a crook and a swindler, the cubs sort of liked him, and the look of things worried them. They put on speed and left a trail of breath puffs as they hurried toward the ice-encrusted houseboat.

• Chapter 7 •

Freezing and Starving!

"Hello, the boat! Hello, the boat!" shouted Brother. There was no sign of life.

"There's no smoke coming from the chimney," said Fred.

"Maybe he's not aboard," said Sister.

Brother shouted again. Still no sign of life.

"Maybe he's dead," said Lizzy with a shiver that was not caused by the cold. "He *said* it was a matter of life and death."

"I think we'd better investigate," said Brother.

The scouts had no more than set foot on

the gangplank when the cabin door opened and a ghostly figure peered out.

Ralph always cut a fine figure in the summer with his snazzy plaid suit and snappy straw hat. But he was a pitiful sight as he looked out of his cabin door. He was pulling his jacket up around his neck for warmth. There were icicles hanging from his hat and his nose. "Thank goodness you've come!" he gasped. "Save me! I'm fading fast!"

The scouts rushed up the gangplank and caught Ralph before he collapsed. They helped him into the cabin and set him down in his easy chair.

"It's freezing in here!" said Brother.

"It's colder in here than it is outside," said Fred. And indeed it was.

"Where's Squawk?" asked Lizzy, looking around the cabin.

"In — in the oven," stuttered Ralph, his teeth chattering clickety-click.

"You cooked your pet parrot?" shrieked Lizzy, rushing to the oven.

"Of course not!" said Ralph. "It's just to keep the poor creature out of this awful wind."

Wind was whistling through holes in the cabin walls. Lizzy opened the oven. Sure enough, there was Squawk, all bundled up in sweaters.

"Sq-sq-sq-squawk!" stuttered Squawk, his beak chattering clickety-click.

"Poor thing!" said Lizzy.

"How about me?" said Ralph.

"How did you come to this?" said Brother, looking around the cabin. He turned to his fellow scouts and said, "Hurry! Go find some sticks to build a fire with."

"It's my own fault," said Ralph. "I delayed going downriver to warmer climes just a little too late and . . . well, you see what happened. I've no money, no food, no firewood. So I'm slowly freezing and starving to death. Please take Squawk to the warmth of one of your cozy homes. There's no hope for me. I can feel the icicles forming round my heart. Farewell, sweet scouts! Farewell!"

"You stop that kind of talk," said Brother. "You can't give up. You've got dozens of crooked swindling years still ahead of you."

The firewood pickings were pretty slim, but they got a small fire going in the stove.

"Is there any way we can help you?" asked Brother.

"I'm beyond help!" cried Ralph. "It's

over for me! I've no visible means of support! There's no one out in this weather. No one to cheat or swindle. And I've just lost my last hope of survival. I've been turned down by Chief Bruno and your estimable father, Papa Q. Bear. Farewell! Farewell! I'm fading fast!"

"Turned down by Papa and the chief," said Sister. "What do you suppose he means?"

Brother shrugged. "What do you mean, turned down by Papa and the chief?" he asked.

Ralph sighed. "When I saw fate closing in on me in the form of this dreadful winter, I asked permission to put up a small gaming booth at the Winter Carnival. Nothing special. Just a small wheel of fortune and perhaps a hoop toss. It might have seen me through the winter. But, alas, they turned me down cold." He was seized by a spasm of shivers.

"Excuse us a minute, Ralph," said Brother. The scouts gathered in a corner of the cabin. "What do you think, guys?"

"You can't blame them for turning him down," said Fred.

"Ralph's famous for his crooked games," said Sister.

"Yes, but he's freezing to death," said Brother. "Look, here's the deal. If Ralph promises to run the games absolutely fair and square, we'll talk to Papa and the chief about letting Ralph in on the Winter Carnival. Deal?"

"Deal," chorused the scouts.

"Promise? Of course I'll promise!" said Ralph when the Scouts told him about the deal. "What choice do I have? Icicles can't be choosers. I promise on my sacred mother's grave! Bless you, my friends. You've warmed my heart. I can feel the blood coursing through my frozen veins. You've saved a life — a worthless life — but a life nonetheless."

"Now, understand. If we can put this over with Papa and the chief, we're going to watch you like a hawk!"

"Four hawks!" said Sister.

"Understood! Understood! Bless you, my friends! Bless you and farewell!"

As soon as the scouts were out the door, Ralph went to the window, cleared a circle of ice, and looked out. As the scouts got back into their skis and poled away, Ralph grinned from ear to ear and said, "Bless you. Bless you, my sucker friends!" Then he turned to Squawk and said, "If I don't hurry and get back to normal, we *will* freeze to death!"

First he removed the icicles from his nose and hat and put them in a box labeled "glass icicles — fragile"; then he took some panels and nailed them over the holes in the walls. Next, he uncovered some logs concealed under a blanket and added them to the fire the scouts had made. Soon the stove was aglow with life-giving warmth.

Ralph eased back in his easy chair. "As the great Phineas T. Bearnum once said of suckers: 'There's one born every minute.' "

"One born every minute!" squawked Squawk. "One born every minute!"

If the scouts, who were silently shussing home, had looked back, they would have seen black wood smoke pouring happily from Ralph's smokestack. But they never looked back.

• Chapter 8 •

Please, Papa, Have a Heart!

"I don't know," said Papa. "Letting Ralph put a wheel of fortune into the Winter Carnival would be like making a fox door guard at the chicken house."

"But, Papa," said Brother. "He's in terrible shape. Icicles on his hat and nose. Wind blowing through the holes in the walls."

The scouts were still warming up with mugs of Mama's best cocoa. Between sips, they pressed Papa to give Ralph a break.

"He has no visible means of support," said Sister.

"He promised on his sacred mother's grave," said Lizzy.

"We'll take responsibility for him," said Brother.

"We'll watch him like a hawk," said Fred.

"Four hawks," said Lizzy.

The scouts could tell Papa was wavering between yes and no.

"Please, Papa," said Sister. "Have a heart!"

"Okay, I'll do it," said Papa. "I'll talk to the chief at the next meeting."

"Do you think he'll go along?" asked Brother.

"Of course he'll go along," said Papa. "I'm Grand Marshal. What I say goes! But remember now — you're going to watch him like a hawk."

"Four hawks," said Brother.

He and the rest of the troop touched cocoa mugs and said, "One for all and all for one!"

• Chapter 9 •

The Crystal Tower

Getting ready for something as big and grand as the Winter Carnival was a lot of work. But the work was going well. A snow fence was put around the carnival grounds. Merry-go-rounds and other rides were brought in and set up. The ski and toboggan runs that the scouts had laid out were flagged and roped off. A mountain of extra snow was trucked in for the snow-sculpture contest. A grandstand was built beside the hockey rink, where the barrel jump would also take place. Coach Grizzmeyer was made referee for all the sports contests, and Mr. Smock, the art teacher, would judge the snow sculptures. After a lot of planning, the biggest project, which was Papa's great ice tower, was beginning to take shape.

Papa, who was a woodworker by trade, knew everything there was to know about working with wood. But there was a big difference between repairing and refinishing one of Lady Grizzly's antique chairs and building a thirty-story tower out of blocks of ice. Papa wasn't shy about seeking help. He got some very good design ideas from Professor Actual Factual, but the professor had some concerns about the safety of a thirty-story tower. So he brought in the firm of T. Square and Plumbob to check out the stress factors. Squire Grizzly brought one of his construction crews in to cut the blocks of ice from the frozen lake and another to build

the tower. It was exciting watching the ice tower climb into the sky.

"It's so beautiful," said Lizzy.

"It looks like cut glass or crystal," said Fred.

"Or frozen diamonds," said Sister

"Hey," said Brother. "Cut glass, crystal, and diamonds are all very well. But aren't we supposed to keep an eye on Ralph?"

"I just checked him out," said Sister. "He's got his wheel of fortune all set up,

and he's working on his hoop toss. He hasn't built in any of his cheating tricks — at least not so far. But you're right. He's our responsibility, and we do have to keep an eye on him."

As it was turning out, there was a lot more to do at the carnival than keep an eye on Ralph. The scouts were spending every day after school and most of Saturday at the carnival grounds. They even stopped by on Sunday. And while they had no regular duties, there was plenty to do. They took the hot-food sled around for the construction crews. They put in the flags for the slalom race. They ran errands for Grand Marshal Papa Q. Bear. They checked passes at the gate.

As the great ice tower climbed higher and higher into the winter sky and opening day got closer and closer, the scouts and everybody else got more and more excited. The big question was, would they have everything ready and in place in time for opening day?

Then, one evening, as the winter sun was about to set, the question was answered. It was almost a miracle, but everything *would* be ready and in place in time for the grand opening of the Winter Carnival the next day at noon.

It was an important moment for the small army of bears who had planned and built the Winter Carnival. They gathered to admire their handiwork and think about the vast army of bears who would pass through the gates the next day. As they looked out at the great ice tower, the great snow mountain brought in for the sculptures, the rides, the hockey rink, the food court, and the ski run and toboggan slide way off in the mountains, they felt good about themselves and the work they had done. But then something happened to put a pall on their expectations of a glorious opening day.

• Chapter 10 •

A Message on Snow Mountain

It was the setting sun that revealed the message on the mountain of snow. It was a familiar message. The scouts recognized it immediately. The twenty-foot-tall letters carved out in the snow said:

Before the crowd could even gasp, a small figure with a raggedy hat, a raggedy suit, and a raggedy beard appeared atop the snow mountain. It was I. M. Weird, the hibernationist. He was speaking through a bullhorn. "REPENT!" he cried. "REPENT OR BE DOOMED! GIVE UP YOUR MODERN WAYS! GO BACK TO THE OLD WAYS! HIBERNATE OR BE DOOMED!"

Talk about a killjoy! Talk about a grouch at the party! The crowd was furious. They started to go after him. "Get him! Get the creep! Run him out of town!"

Chief Bruno blew a blast on his police whistle. "Stop!" he roared. He, too, had a bullhorn. "I'll deal with this. YOU'RE TRESPASSING, SIR. COME DOWN FROM THERE!"

"REPENT!" cried the hibernationist. "HIBERNATE OR BE DOOMED!"

It had become a battle of the bullhorns, with the chief ordering Weird down off the

mountain of snow and Weird crying, "Repent or be doomed!" When Weird was satisfied that he'd gotten his message across, he came down off the mountain. Chief Bruno took him in charge and conducted him to the gate.

It was easy to scoff at the weird Mr. Weird. But once you scoffed, you were left with a nagging feeling that maybe something awful *was* about to happen.

"ATTENTION, PLEASE!" It was Chief Bruno on his bullhorn again. "WE'RE GOING TO LEAVE NOW! AND *NOBODY* — REPEAT *NOBODY* — WILL ENTER THESE GROUNDS UNTIL NINE O'CLOCK TOMORROW MORNING. THERE WILL BE NO EXCEPTIONS. THAT WILL GIVE US THREE HOURS TO GET READY FOR THE TWELVE NOON GRAND OPENING!"

"Talk about weird," said Scout Brother as they left the grounds.

"Talk about I. M. Weird," said Sister, accompanying him to the gate.

• **Chapter 11** •

Ralph on Ice

Ralph slept fitfully that night. He had a great deal to do the next morning, and he had to do it before nine o'clock. He woke with the first rays of dawn. The red coals of his night fire matched the fiery edge of the rising sun. He rose and stoked the fire, fed Squawk, changed from his pajamas into his clothes, had a quick breakfast, and put on his ice skates.

It would have taken more than an hour of strenuous cross-country skiing to reach the carnival grounds overland. But there was just a mile or so of frozen river to

where it joined Lake Grizzly and the site
of the Winter Carnival. Ralph made good
time, even carrying the case of "attach-
ments" he would add to his so-called
games of chance. Visions of large stacks of
money danced in his greedy mind as he
thought about all the planes, trains, and
automobiles streaking toward Beartown
filled with suckers.

Soon he was off the ice, out of his
skates, and hard at work on his games. He

added a foot pedal to the wheel of fortune. It would let him control the wheel so that nobody could win. He was in the middle of win-proofing the hoop toss when he chanced to look out of his booth and see something strange and scary coming over the horizon. It was some sort of moving figure. It was terrifying even in the distance. As it came closer it was terrifying beyond words; it froze his blood and drove everything from his mind but one word.

What was that word? It was *doom. Doom!*
DOOM! Ralph ran screaming from his
booth.

• Chapter 12 •

Awfully Early for Screaming and Hollering

"Wow! This is some breakfast," said Brother. There was honey-baked salmon, bugleberry jam, homemade nut bread, milk for the cubs, and sassafras tea for Mama and Papa.

"Yum!" agreed Sister.

"All in honor, no doubt, of the grand opening of the Winter Carnival just hours hence," said Papa. "The Winter Carnival of which yours truly, Papa Q. Bear, is Grand Marshal."

"Nonsense," said Mama. "It's just that

once things get rolling you won't have time for a decent meal."

Brother started to say something but stopped in the middle and cocked his ear. "What's that noise? Sounds like some sort of screaming and hollering."

"My goodness," said Mama. "It's awfully early in the morning for screaming and hollering. The sun's barely up. It'll wake the whole neighborhood."

They opened the front door and went out to the stoop. "It's Ralph," said Brother. "I can't make out what he's saying, but one thing's for sure. Something has scared him out of his wits."

"Look," said Mama. "He *has* wakened the whole neighborhood."

"Come on!" said Papa. "Let's meet him halfway."

Scouts Lizzy and Fred were among the neighbors who gathered around the blithering, blathering, hysterical Ralph.

Whatever had scared Ralph was pouring out in a crazy mixed-up jumble.

"Please calm down, Ralph!" said Papa. "We can't understand what you're saying!" But while Papa and the others fussed at Ralph, Scout Fred listened hard to the jumble.

"Excuse me," said Fred. "I think I know what he's trying to tell us."

"Well, for Pete's sake tell *us*!" said Papa.

"As nearly as I can figure it out," said Fred, "he's saying we're all doomed just like that Mr. Weird said, and that some sort of monster has come. And it's over at the carnival grounds right this minute."

By now Ralph had collapsed. He was sitting on the snow, gasping and twitching.

"Is that what you're talking about, Ralph?" said Fred. "A monster?"

Ralph shook his head and gasped, "Ice monster."

The crowd looked at Grand Marshal Papa for leadership.

"To the carnival grounds!" roared Papa after a moment's hesitation. "And let's not go empty-handed!"

The crowd picked up rocks, boards, and clubs as they raced to the carnival grounds — and possible doom.

• Chapter 13 •

The Doomsday Monster

The crowd stopped dead in its tracks
when it arrived at the carnival grounds.
There, shambling among the rides and
booths, was the biggest, weirdest monster
ever seen outside of nightmares and hor-
ror movies. It wasn't just that it was

weird-looking. It was weird-looking with a capital WEIRD! It was as though a gigantic frozen corn shock with arms and legs had come to life and was looking for something to tear apart. It didn't seem to have any face. Or at least what face it had was all straw and icicles.

The monster must have had eyes somewhere in that straw and icicle head because it turned and looked at the crowd. It was a look that could turn blood to ice. It was touch-and-go whether the crowd would turn and run, freeze where it was, or advance to what looked like certain doom.

Once again the crowd was looking to Grand Marshal Papa for leadership. The Bear Scouts gathered around Papa and urged him on. "Come on, Papa!" cried Brother. "We've got him outnumbered a hundred to one!"

"Yes," said Papa. "But he's got us out-uglied a thousand to one!"

For a second it was a standoff. But then a small movement of retreat by the monster lent courage to Papa and the crowd. "After him!" cried Papa. "Let's show him what doomsday's all about!"

The monster took one look at all those

rocks, boards, and clubs and shambled away.

"Look!" cried Scout Fred. "He's heading for the ice tower!"

"Good grief!" cried Brother. "He's climbing the ice tower!"

It was quite a scene: the hideous, big-as-a-house ice monster climbing the great ice tower, the crazed crowd gathered at its base waving their weapons. The noisy arrival of Chief Bruno and Officer Marguerite on snowmobiles just added to the confusion.

"We've got a monster problem, Chief," said Papa. "But I've got an idea. There's only one individual who can go up against that monster, and that's Bigpaw! Let me borrow one of your snowmobiles and I'll fetch him."

"But Bigpaw's hibernating," protested Sister. "There's no telling what'll happen if you try to wake a hibernating bear —

especially a bear as big and powerful as Bigpaw!"

"I'll just have to take that chance," cried Papa. He hopped onto the snowmobile and roared off toward the mountains.

"Chief," said Scout Fred. "Do you have a cell phone?"

"Right here," said the chief.

"Then I have a suggestion," said Fred. "This is a perfect chance for Professor Actual Factual to try out his latest invention. It's a biplane with a wing-mounted tranquilizer machine gun rigged to shoot through the propeller."

"Good thinking," said the chief. He punched in the professor's number and spoke into the phone.

Meanwhile, the ice monster was climbing, climbing, climbing up the great ice tower.

• Chapter 14 •

In Bigpaw's Cave

Papa had parked the chief's snowmobile at the foot of the Great Grizzly Mountains and climbed the rest of the way to Bigpaw's cave. It hadn't been easy. There had been a lot of slipping and sliding, barked shins, and skinned knees. But Papa was urged on by desperation. The doomsday monster was not only a threat to all Bear Country, but with the grand opening just hours away it could completely mess up Grand Marshal Papa's beautiful Winter Carnival.

As Papa prepared to enter the cave, he

remembered Sister's warning about the dangers of trying to waken a hibernating bear — especially a bear as big and powerful as Bigpaw. But that was the whole point! Only a bear as big and powerful as Bigpaw could take on the doomsday monster.

The cave's yawning mouth was guarded by rows of jagged icicle teeth. Grand Marshal or not, Papa was scared. It was as dark and spooky inside as a dragon's throat. Papa looked back across the snow-covered valley and saw his beautiful Winter Carnival in the distance. It was glistening pink in the risen sun, and — good grief — there was the monster atop his beautiful tower. He had to go on.

Papa switched on the chief's flashlight and pointed it into the darkness. Blizzard winds had drifted snow onto the cave floor. "Bigpaw," said Papa softly as he entered the cave. "Oh, Bigpaw. It's me, Papa Q.

Bear. We're having some trouble, and we need a little help. Don't be frightened. It's your friend, Papa Q. Bear."

Papa finally reached Bigpaw's hibernation bed deep at the rear of the cave. It was empty! Bigpaw was gone!

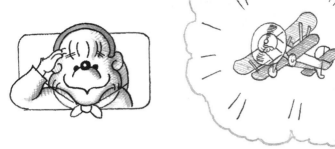

• Chapter 15 •

A Big Target

Chief Bruno and Officer Marguerite were trying to manage the crowd. They were getting ready for Professor Actual Factual's tranquilizer attack by clearing the area at the base of the tower.

"Move back, please. And put down your weapons," said the chief. "Everything's under control. Professor Actual Factual's flying in with a tranquilizer gun."

"How're you gonna tranquilize an ice monster?" said one construction worker. The tough construction gang had arrived.

They wanted to get ladders and go after the monster.

"Hey, we're the law here," said the chief. "Move 'em back, Marguerite."

Scout Brother was scanning the sky with the chief's field glasses.

"Do you see him yet?" asked Fred.

"Not yet, not yet," said Brother. "Hey, wait. I think I've got him. Yep, it's gotta be the professor's biplane. Here, take a look." Fred took the field glasses.

"Yes, it's definitely the professor," said Fred. "I can make out the tranquilizer gun on the wing."

"I don't know about this tranquilizer business," said Lizzy, who was so into nature that she even worried about monsters.

Sister and Lizzy were best friends, but they sometimes got on each other's nerves. Today was Sister's turn to be irritated. "I just don't get you sometimes, Lizzy," complained Sister. "I mean, kindness to animals is one thing. But worrying about that hideous, dangerous, disgusting creature is another."

"All I'm saying is I'm worried about that — what did Fred call it? A tranquilizer *machine* gun. Sounds pretty scary to me. Besides," said Lizzy, "how do we know he's dangerous?"

"How do we know he's dangerous?" said Sister. "Just look at him! Anything that weird-looking has *got* to be dangerous!"

"A rhinoceros beetle is pretty weird-looking," said Lizzy. "But it's not the least bit dangerous."

"That thing on the tower is a *billion* times bigger than a rhinoceros beetle. Oh, I give up!" said Sister.

"Oh, I don't think you have to worry, Lizzy," said Fred. "Actual Factual wouldn't hurt a fly. He wants to study the monster, not hurt him."

"He might hurt a fly that big," said Sister.

The professor's plane was now overhead. The chief was trying to contact him on the two-way radio. "Come in, Professor. Chief Bruno here. Come in, Professor . . ."

"Actual Factual here," said the professor in a crackly radio voice. "I'm getting ready to make my first pass. I want to avoid hitting a vital part. I'm going to try for a rump shot."

"At least he's got a big target," said Sister.

"Is there any danger he'll come crashing down?" asked the chief. "A thing that size could do a lot of damage."

"No danger of that," crackled the professor. "I'm using a combination of slow-acting tranquilizer and something that will give him acrophobia."

"That's fear of heights," explained Fred.

"So he ought to come down on his own," said the professor. "And be out by the time he reaches the ground. Okay, I'm going to make my first pass. Here I go! . . ."

All eyes turned up to see the professor go into a slanting dive. But the monster shifted as the professor came in close — a little too close — and the plane's landing gear brushed the monster, leaving a flash of red at the monster's shoulder.

"Oh, you've wounded him! You've wounded him!" cried Lizzy.

"I don't think so," said Sister, peering

through the field glasses.

"Come in, Professor," said the chief. "Did you hit him?"

"Actual Factual here," answered the professor. "Yes, I'm afraid I did, but not with the tranquilizer gun. I'm going in for another shot."

"No, hold everything!" cried Sister. "Tell him to stop!"

"Stop — repeat, stop, Professor," said the chief. "What's your problem, Sister?"

"Here, see for yourself," said Sister. She handed Chief Bruno the field glasses.

"Hey," said the chief. "That's not a wound. It's a big red bow around the neck of a . . . TEDDY BEAR?"

The monster shifted again. But this time he lost his grip and began to slide bumpety-bump down the ice tower. By the time he hit bottom he'd lost most of the straw, sticks, snow, and icicles he'd brought with him from his hibernation bed.

Chief Bruno was completely nonplussed. All he could say was, "But . . . But . . . But . . ."

"Don't you get it, Chief?" cried Sister. "It's Bigpaw!"

"But why was he all got up like a monster?" said the chief. "And where did he get that teddy?"

"That monster stuff was just his hibernation bed all stuck to him," explained Brother. "As for the teddy, we gave it to him as a hibernation present."

"I still don't get it," said the chief, scratching his head.

"I think I know what happened," said Fred. "We told Bigpaw about the Winter Carnival when we gave him the teddy. I think what happened was that he dreamed about it and it seemed like so much fun that he sleepwalked over here."

"Are you trying to tell me that Bigpaw *sleepwalked* from his cave to the carnival?" said the chief.

"I think it's pretty obvious, Chief," said Brother. Bigpaw was beginning to stir.

"Hello, Bigpaw," said Sister. "It's me, Sister Bear." Bigpaw looked confused.

That's when Papa roared up on the snowmobile shouting, "Bigpaw wasn't in his cave! Bigpaw wasn't in his cave!" When he saw Bigpaw sitting at the foot of the ice tower hugging his teddy, Papa was *really* confused. "Huh? What are *you* doing here, Bigpaw?"

"That's what Bigpaw want to know," said Bigpaw. "What I doing here?"

• Chapter 16 •
You Win Some, You Lose Some

There was no question that getting ready
for the Winter Carnival took a miracle.
But given the events of the morning, opening on time took an even bigger miracle.
But open they did. And the way things
worked out, Grand Marshal Papa's Winter
Carnival was an even bigger success than
he had hoped it would be. The crowds
were enormous. They rode the rides, en-
joyed the competitions, ate the food, and
lined up for the hot cocoa. They "oohed"
and "aahed" at Papa's magnificent ice
tower. But, as it turned out, the biggest

attraction was Bigpaw himself. He shook hands, kissed babies, and signed autographs.

He still wasn't quite sure how he got to the carnival, but he and his teddy were loving every minute of it. The scouts tried

to explain about the dream and the sleep-walking, but Bigpaw was too excited to listen. The scouts were happy to let it go at that.

Things went beautifully that first day. There were congratulations all around for Grand Marshal Papa Q. Bear. He had done himself proud. Even Mama had to admit Papa's Winter Carnival was a triumph.

There was one bit of trouble. It happened when wily Farmer Ben peeked under the curtain and discovered Ralph's wheel of fortune was fixed.

"The wheel is fixed!" cried Farmer Ben. "He's got a foot pedal under there!"

"You don't understand, Ben," said Ralph. "This foot pedal . . ."

"I understand perfectly, you miserable crook!" Farmer Ben bent down to make a snowball. Ralph beat a fast retreat, but it wasn't fast enough. Ben's snowball was right on target. Some visitors who had also gotten cheated decided to try out *their* pitching arms. But Ralph was fast, and he was almost out of range when Bigpaw happened along.

"Ooh! Snowballs!" said Bigpaw. "Bigpaw like throw snowballs!" He made a really big one and let it fly. It sailed through the air like a big fluffy white cannonball. It landed squarely on Ralph, foiling his escape.

"What's going on here?" said the chief, who'd heard there was trouble at Ralph's booth. "Hmmm, no explanation needed," said the chief when he saw the foot pedal.

"Aren't you going to take him in, Chief?" asked Brother.

"No," said Chief Bruno with a smile. "I think I'll just let him cool his heels for a while."

The scouts joined the chief as he continued his tour of the carnival.

"It's been quite a day, hasn't it, Chief?" said Brother.

"It certainly has," agreed the chief. "And I'll admit it, when I first saw that 'monster' I figured we were doomed just like that raggedy Mr. Weird said. Say, I wonder what happened to him."

"Right here," said weird little Mr. Weird. "I. M. Weird at your service."

"Well, hello," said the chief. "Do you mind if I ask you a question?"

"Not at all," said Mr. Weird.

"About all those predictions and warnings about hibernation and doom," said the chief. "Well, they haven't exactly worked out. How do you feel about that?"

I. M. Weird shrugged. "Hey," he said. "You win some, you lose some. Now, if you'll excuse me, I'm going to ride on the merry-go-round."

And he did.

• About the Authors •

Stan and Jan Berenstain have been writing and illustrating books about bears for more than thirty years. Their very first book about the Bear Scout characters was published in 1967. Through the years the Bear Scouts have done their best to defend the weak, catch the crooked, joust against the unjust, and rally against rottenness of all kinds. In fact, the scouts have done such a great job of living up to the Bear Scout Oath, the authors say, that "they deserve a series of their own."

Stan and Jan Berenstain live in Bucks County, Pennsylvania. They have two sons, Michael and Leo, and four grandchildren. Michael is an artist, and Leo is a writer. Michael did the pictures in this book.

Don't Miss

THE *Berenstain* BEAR SCOUTS
and the
Really Big Disaster

At first, Bigpaw seemed to fit right in on his new job. There were mountains of building materials at the building site: steel rods, concrete blocks, piles of lumber, coils of cable, great steel girders. The squire's foreman, Otto McFurback, started Bigpaw on moving these heavy materials to where they were needed: tons of brick, vats of mortar, truckloads of flooring material.

As Bigpaw gained confidence, he began doing things on his own. The first real trouble came when Bigpaw observed that wheelbarrowing the cement from the cement mixer to where it was being poured into wooden forms was a very slow process. Bigpaw figured it would save a lot of time if he ripped the mixer off its truck and used it like a pitcher to fill the forms. So that's what he did. It saved a lot of time, but it didn't go over so well with the owner of the rented cement-mixer truck.

"My truck! My truck!" cried the owner. "That monster has destroyed it!"

The squire's foreman calmed him down. But it *was* a great time-saver. The foreman suggested that instead of tearing the mixer off the truck, he pick up the whole truck and use *it* like a pitcher. Now Bigpaw was really into the swing of things. When the job came to a stop because they'd run out of sewer pipe, Bigpaw saved the day (or so he thought) by ripping out some extra pipe he found buried in the ground.

But the pipe wasn't extra at all. It was part of the town water-main system. Water squirted in every direction. It flooded the job site. It shut off the water in every pipe, sink, and toilet in Beartown. It caused short circuits in the electrical system. Sparks flew from the overheard wires. The cry went up, "Somebody turn off the electricity!" But it was a dangerous situation. There was no way anybody could go near the wires. Nobody except Bigpaw. He reached down and pulled two of the poles completely out of the ground. Then he raised the two poles high over his head and snapped the wires they carried. That turned off the electricity, all right. It turned it off all over Beartown. It also pulled down rows and rows of utility poles. The whole Beartown business district was a flooded tangle of downed poles and wet wire, not to mention a small army of fighting-mad businessbears.